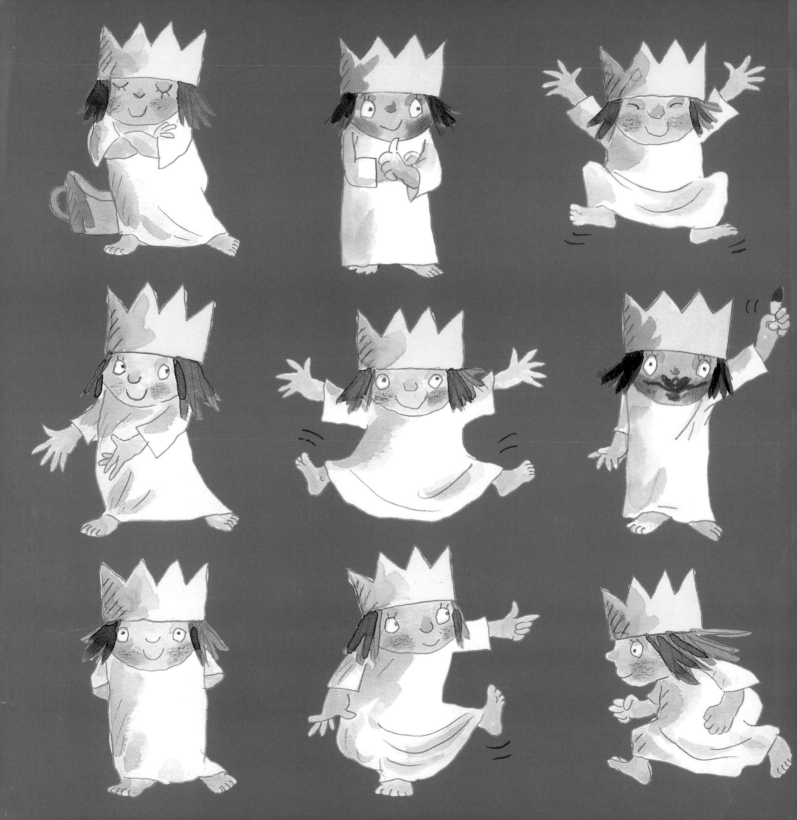

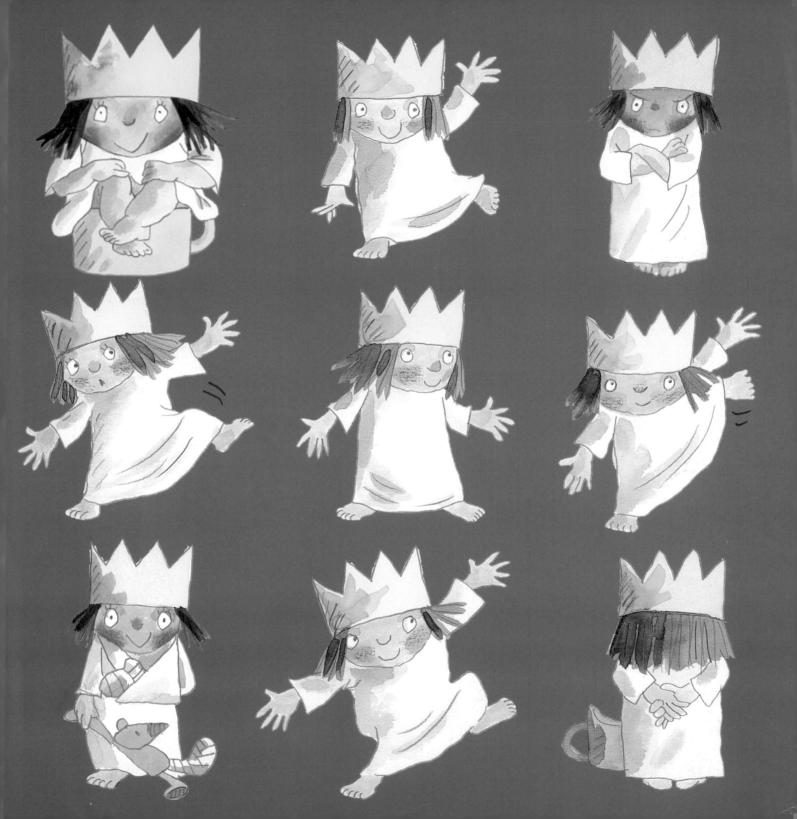

This edition produced for The Book People Ltd,
Hall Wood Avenue, Haydock, St Helens WA11 9UL

First published in hardback in Great Britain by Andersen Press Ltd in 2002
First published in paperback by Collins Picture Books in 2004

ISBN-13: 978-0-00-778929-0
ISBN-10: 0-00-778929-7

Collins Picture Books is an imprint of the Children's Division, part of HarperCollins Publishers Ltd.

Text and illustrations copyright © Tony Ross 2002

The author/illustrator asserts the moral right to be identified as the author/illustrator of the work.

A CIP catalogue record for this title is available from the British Library.

Visit our website at: www.harpercollinschildrensbooks.co.uk

Printed and bound in Hong Kong by Printing Express Ltd.

Colour Reproduction by Dot Gradations Ltd, UK

I Want My Tooth

Tony Ross

HarperCollins *Children's Books*

The Little Princess had WONDERFUL teeth.

She counted them every morning.
Then she cleaned them . . .

. . . then she counted them again.
She had TWENTY.

Some of her friends had fewer than twenty teeth.
But THEY were not ROYAL.

Her little brother, who WAS royal,
had NO teeth at all.

"Haven't I got wonderful teeth?" said the Little Princess.
"In smart straight lines," said the General.
"Shipshape and Bristol fashion," said the Admiral.

"Haven't I got wonderful teeth?" said the Little Princess.
"ROYAL teeth!" said the King.

So every night, the Little Princess cleaned
the royal teeth again.

"Your wonderful teeth are because you eat all the right things," said the Cook.

"You can count them if you like," said the Little Princess.
"One . . . two . . . three . . . four . . .

"HEY," said the Cook. "This one WOBBLES!"

"AAAAAGH!" screamed the Little Princess.
"One WOBBLES!"

"AAAAAGH!" screamed the Maid.
"One WOBBLES!"

The wobbly tooth wobbled MORE each day.

But the wobbly tooth didn't hurt, and soon
the Little Princess enjoyed wobbling it.

And she wobbled it and wobbled it, until the terrible day the wobbly tooth disappeared.

"I WANT MY TOOTH!"
cried the Little Princess.

"You can have mine," said the Dentist,
"until your new one comes along!"
"I want my tooth NOW!" said the Little Princess.

Everybody in the Palace searched for the missing tooth . . .

. . . but it was NOWHERE to be found.
"I WANT MY TOOTH!" cried the Little Princess.

"SHE WANTS HER TOOTH!" cried the Maid.

"It's all right," said the Little Princess.
"I've FOUND it . . .

. . . HE'S got it!"

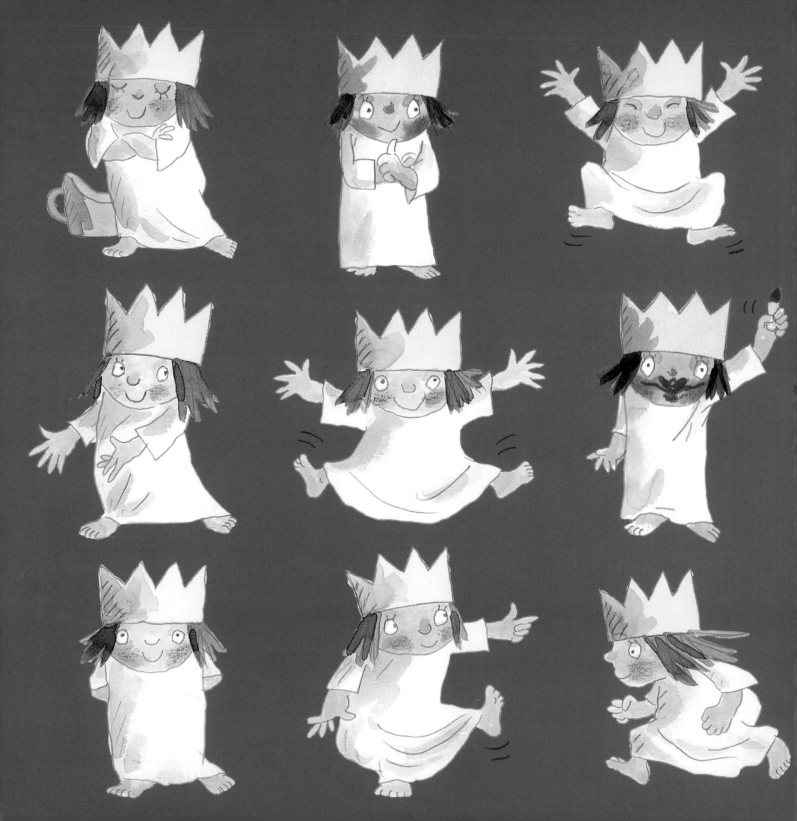

Collect all the funny stories featuring the demanding Little Princess!

0-00-662687-4

0-00-664357-4

0-00-664356-6

0-00-664730-8

0-00-710957-1

0-00-712298-5

0-00-715072-5

Tony Ross was born in London in 1938. His dream was to work with horses but instead he went to art college in Liverpool. Since then, Tony has worked as an art director at an advertising agency, a graphic designer, a cartoonist, a teacher and a film maker – as well as illustrating over 250 books! Tony, his wife Zoe and family live in Macclesfield, Cheshire.